Pearl's Dressing-Up Dreams

The Frilly Nightdress

JENNY OLDFIELD

Illustrated by Dawn Apperley

Hodder Children's Books

A division of Hachette Children's Books

Pearl sat on the big dressing-up box in Amber's basement.

"Why don't you want to play at dressing up?" Amber demanded. "We usually do!"

"I don't feel like it today," Pearl shrugged. She kicked her heels against the side of the box.

"Is it because you're scared of Wolfie?" Lily asked quietly. "Don't get me wrong,

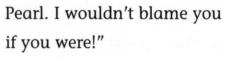

Pearl. I wouldn't blame you if you were!"

Pearl remembered the Wolf's big teeth and flashing eyes, and how he followed her everywhere she went. "No, it's not that," she sighed.

"So why then?" Amber asked again. "I thought you liked the little cottage near the woods where Red Riding-Hood lives . . ."

"And whatisname – Hans, the boy next door," Lily interrupted.

"And those cool talking animals," Amber reminded Pearl.

"I do, I do!" Pearl wished they would leave her alone. There again, she knew it

6

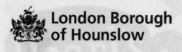

The Satin Dress
The Diamond Tiara
The Velvet Cloak
The Glass Slippers

The Silver Mirror
The Flowered Apron
The Pearly Comb
The Lace Gown

The Red Cloak
The Party Frock
The Picnic Basket
The Frilly Nightdress

wasn't really Amber and Lily's fault – after all she'd been the one who'd gone on and on about wanting a turn at whooshing off into the magic dressing-up world.

And so far she'd loved every minute – well, *almost* every minute of Red Riding-Hood world. But right here, right now, she didn't fancy going back.

"Are you really scared of Wolfie?" Amber asked, sitting next to Pearl on the box. "I mean, we're almost at the part where he dresses up in your gran's nightie and tries to scoff you!"

"Yeah, thanks for that, Amber!" Lily tutted. "Now Pearl definitely won't do any more dressing up."

But Pearl jumped down from the box and shook her head. "Honestly, it's not that. I'd go back, no problem, if it was just Wolfie I was worried about. But if you really want to know the truth, it's Hannah."

"Red Riding-Hood's cousin?" Lily thought this through. "That doesn't make sense, Pearl. What's scary about a little kid?"

"A *pretty* little kid with long golden curls," Amber reminded her. "Who suddenly appears out of nowhere, and everyone says, 'How cute!' and 'Isn't she sweet?'"

"Oh – yeah." Lily got the point. Pearl was jealous of the new arrival. "Sorry, Pearl, I forgot."

Pearl frowned and went to the window to look out at the rain. "How mean does

8

that make me look!"

Then she remembered her friend, Ratty, who had helped to save her life, and the wonderful stag and the cute rabbits and squirrels who had come to her picnic in the wood. She made up her mind and turned back to Amber and Lily. "OK, so I'm a little bit scared of Wolfie," she admitted. "And I am a teeny-weeny bit jealous of Hannah."

"Just a smidge!" Amber grinned.

"But I'm over it," Pearl declared, throwing open the lid of Amber's dressing-up box. "Let me in. I want to get whooshed back there as soon as ever I can!"

"No – no – no!" Pearl tried on an orange skirt, a black beret and a pair of silver ballet pumps. Nothing worked. She was still standing in Amber's basement.

"Try these." Lily offered her a Mickey Mouse mask and a pair of big white gloves.

"Forget it. Have a sweet instead," Amber said, offering Pearl a mint humbug.

Pearl took two and popped one in her mouth. She dug deep into the bottom of the box and pulled out a frilly white nightdress.

"My mum bought it when we all went to Disney World," Amber recalled. "Try it on, Pearl. Let's see what happens."

So Pearl sucked the sweet and pulled the nightdress over her head.

"How do you feel?" Lily asked eagerly. "Anything?"

"A teeny bit dizzy." Pearl saw a glimmering light surround her. "Whoa!"

"Hurray, here we go!" Amber cried.

The light grew brighter and warm air filled the room. A gust lifted Pearl off her feet.

"Good luck!" Amber and Lily crossed their fingers.

The light dazzled them. The wind whooshed Pearl away.

Someone was sobbing.

Pearl tried to make out where she was but the room was dark. Outside the window, the wind blew and a branch tapped at the pane.

Sob-sob-sob-sob! A child's heart was breaking.

"What is it? What's wrong?" Pearl asked in the darkness. She made out a mattress on the floor next to her bed, and a shape lying on the mattress, underneath a patchwork quilt.

Sob-swallow! The crying stopped.

"Hannah?" Pearl asked softly.

There was no answer, so Pearl got out of bed.

Tap-tap went the branch at the window. Pearl shuddered. "Hannah?" she whispered.

A fair head appeared from under a corner of the quilt. "Sorry I woke you up," a little voice said.

"It's all right – you didn't. Why are you crying, Hannah? What's wrong?"

There was a long pause before Pearl felt

Hannah's small hand slip into hers. "I miss my mummy," she said at last. "She's gone away and I'm frightened I won't see her ever again!"

"Your mum will come back, don't worry," Pearl had told Hannah, offering her the humbug she found on her pillow. She snuggled her back in her bed. Before long, golden-haired Hannah had fallen asleep.

But Pearl had lain awake, hoping she was right. *Why did Hannah have to come here? Mum only went on a quick visit to her sister, Gertie. So what happened?*

At breakfast the next morning, Hannah looked pale. "When will Mummy come back?" she asked.

Pearl's plump mum bustled around the kitchen, buttering bread and spoon-feeding baby Tommy. "Soon," she soothed, tempting Hannah with a bowl of porridge. "Try not to worry. She has work to do, making a gown for a fine lady in town. She will be back as soon as she can."

Pearl was halfway through her own bowl of porridge when the cottage door flew open and Hans breezed in.

"Have you heard the news from the castle?" he cried, his face flushed and his fair curls blown back from his face.

"No," Pearl replied.

"Da-dah! The news is – the Duchess has gone!"

Pearl's mum dropped her wooden spoon. "What do you mean?" she cried. "When? Where? Why has she gone?"

Hans grinned. "Gone – last night, before sunset! Gone – back to her mother's house beyond the mountain! Gone – because she had a fight with the Duke and swore she didn't love him any more! *Abracadabra* – vanished!"

Pearl pushed her bowl away. "Why are you smiling? If this is true, it's not funny!"

"True as I stand here," Hans insisted. "I came straight down from the castle to bring the news. I have to run and tell your grandmamma that the Duchess has taken Max with her."

16

"So – the Duke has no wife and your grandmother has lost her job in the nursery!" Pearl's mother shook her head and sighed. "I see hard times ahead."

"The castle is in a pickle," Hans reported. "The Duke storms down corridors looking for people to throw into the dungeons. The horses and dogs are not fed, the servants are frightened of their own shadows."

Pearl nodded then reached for her red cloak. "I get the picture. You're right, Hans – we'd better find Gran. I'll come with you."

"What about you, Hannah?" Hans waited in the doorway. "Will you come and see your grandmother?"

Shyly Hannah nodded and climbed

down from her stool.

"Look after her!" Pearl's mum called as they set off across the meadow.

"'There was an old lady who swallowed a fly!'" Hans sang as he and Pearl lifted Hannah over the stile leading to the woods.

"'I don't know why she swallowed the fly – Perhaps she'll die!'"

"It's dark in here," Hannah whispered, peering ahead. "The trees are scary!"

"Don't worry, you're safe with Hans and me," Pearl promised. She hoped they'd get to her grandmother's cottage before the old lady set off for the castle on a wasted journey. "Look at the squirrels up there – aren't they cute?"

"Good morning, Red Riding-Hood!" the

squirrels chattered from their high branch. "It's a lovely day for a picnic!"

"Sorry, no picnics today," Pearl called back over her shoulder as she, Hannah and Hans hurried on through the wood.

"'I know an old lady who swallowed a spider. That wriggled and tickled and tickled inside her. She swallowed the spider to catch the fly. But I don't know why she swallowed the fly – Perhaps she'll die!'"

Hannah pulled a face. "I don't like that song."

"Me neither." Pearl dug Hans with her elbow. "Lighten up, Hans. Sing something that doesn't involve people eating each other!"

"I'm only trying to be cheerful to keep

your minds off Wolfie," he retorted, striding on ahead. "The servants at the castle warned me that he came down from the mountain last night, looking for his supper."

Pearl shivered. She glanced around at the thick bushes and tangle of undergrowth. Then she looked up at a woodpecker clinging to a tree. "Have you seen Wolfie?" she asked anxiously.

Toc-toc-toc! The woodpecker drilled his beak against the tree. "No sign of the Wolf

since dawn!" he reported.

"And you?" Pearl asked the green frog squatting under a broad leaf by a stream. "Have you seen Wolfie pass this way?"

The frog blinked and croaked, "Not this morning."

"See, we're quite safe," Pearl told Hannah, thanking the frog and walking on. "The people at the castle must have got it wrong!"

Little do they know! Wolfie thought. He lay low in his favourite den by the riverbank. *I crept here by night and now I lie in wait. I don't move a muscle. No one knows I'm here!*

The silver river ran on quietly. The leaves on the trees rustled in the breeze. Wolfie licked his lips and waited.

3

"Hurry up, slow-coaches!" Hans told Pearl and Hannah.

They had reached the edge of the wood and their grandmother's cottage was in sight, just beyond the old flour mill.

"We're going as fast as we can." Pearl helped Hannah over a trickling stream. "Hold on, Hans. Will you let me tell Gran the news?"

"What news is this?" said Gran, suddenly appearing from behind the mill. She was dressed up in her posh castle dress of purple silk, with wide petticoats and her best black cloak. "But be quick and tell me your story, or else I'll be late for work."

Pearl took a deep breath. "That's just it," she began. Once she'd started she realised she didn't quite know how to deliver the bad news. "It's – er – about Max and your – er – job at the castle . . ."

"Her Grace the Duchess has upped and left His Grace the Duke!" Hans cut in. "She took baby Max with her, and that's that!"

Pearl and Hannah's gran threw up her hands in horror. "Oh my poor baby!" she cried. "And poor me! What will I do?"

Gran's sobs were as loud as everything else about her. Mice ran for shelter under the mill floor and the ducks on the pond took off in fright.

"No one understands His Baby Grace the way I do!" Gran wailed. "I know when he needs to be fed and when he's teething. Only I can make him smile!"

"Come on, Gran – let me make you a cup of tea," Pearl said, giving Hans a dirty look. "You could've broken it to her more gently," she muttered.

They all trudged back to Gran's cottage, where the old lady soon came round. "This will blow over," she decided, wiping her face with a large handkerchief. "The Duke will beg forgiveness and plead for the Duchess to come home. Max will be back in my arms by this time tomorrow!"

"We hope you're right," Hans said. "The Duke is in a black mood, the whole castle is in disarray. And even though the Duchess can be proud and spiteful, I wish she were home and all was back to normal."

"So, Hannah," Gran said, sniffing and putting away her hankie. "How do you like staying with your cousin?"

"Very well," Hannah answered shyly.

"And is Red Riding-Hood kind to you?" Gran asked, inviting her youngest granddaughter to sit on her knee.

"Yes. She gave me a humbug and she lets me use her quilt to keep warm."

"That's nice. And shall you come often to visit your grandmamma while you stay close by?"

"Every day!" Hannah promised sweetly.

"You're a dear child!" The old lady hugged Hannah. She was thoughtful as Pearl buttoned Hannah's short jacket, ready to go. "Now that I have time on my hands, I have decided to make you a present," she murmured.

"You hear that?" Pearl said. "Grandmamma promises to make you something nice."

"What will it be?" Hannah said, smiling for the first time. She tugged at her grandmother's broad skirt. "What will you make for me?"

"It's a surprise!" Gran replied, picking

up Hannah and hugging her again before she said goodbye. "You must wait until I bring it, which will be tonight, before the sun sets."

Happily Hannah set off with Hans and Pearl. They held her hands and swung her along the path towards the woods.

"Take good care of her!" Gran called after them. "She's very young and there are dangers everywhere!"

"On guard!" Hans cried. He wielded a long stick like a sword. *Swish-swish!* He flashed the stick through the air then marched through the wood ahead of the two girls. "I'm a soldier sent to guard Miss Hannah. Left-right, left-right!"

"Let's march," Pearl said. "Left-right,

left-right, left-right!"

Hannah joined in the game, laughing and marching along.

From his lair by the river, Wolfie spotted Hannah's golden curls and chubby arms. "Tasty!" he muttered, then licked his lips.

He stood up and stretched himself. *A tender morsel for my breakfast. There's nothing I would like better!*

Hans led Hannah and Pearl along the narrow path.

"I like this game," Hannah said. "Left-right, left-right!"

Pearl was enjoying it too. She loved the dappled sunlight falling across the forest floor and the tiny purple flowers peeping

through the long grass. And she was glad that Hannah was happy.

How mean was I to be jealous, she thought, finding a stick for Hannah and stripping it bare to turn it into a sword. *It turns out she's homesick and missing her mum, which I totally understand!*

"'The grand old Duke of York . . .'" Hans

sang a marching song. "'He had ten thousand men . . .'" *Swish-swish* went his sword through the long grass.

"Hi!" Pearl called to the three baby rabbits hopping along the path ahead of them. "It's me – Red Riding-Hood. Won't you stop to talk?"

But the rabbits were in a hurry. "Our mother's calling from our burrow," they explained, darting into the bushes.

"'He marched them up to the top of the hill . . .'" Hans sang.

"What about you?" Pearl asked the squirrels, peering down at her from the branches. "Will you join our game?"

"Not today," they replied. "Our father told us we must not leave the treetops."

What's going on? Pearl wondered,

beginning to look around more carefully.

"'And he marched them down again!'" Hans marched on.

"Hang on a minute!" Pearl called him back. She held tight to Hannah's hand. "Something's not right. The rabbits and squirrels don't want to play."

Wolfie crouched low behind a thorn bush. His yellow eyes glittered. *I'll have the small child for my breakfast and Red Riding-Hood for lunch, then I'll gobble down the boy for supper!*

He moved forward without a sound.

"What's wrong?" Hannah asked in a quavery voice. She could tell Pearl was worried, and she didn't think the woods were such fun now that the sun had gone behind the clouds and left them in shadow.

"Nothing." Pearl tried to sound brave. "Let's walk on as fast as we can."

"Don't be scared!" Hans declared, raising his sword-stick high in the air. "If the Wolf comes, I'll save you!"

"Typical!" Pearl sighed. "I wasn't going to mention Wolfie, in case it scared her," she whispered to Hans.

"Is there a wolf in this wood?" Hannah wailed, clutching Pearl's hand. "Where is he? Will he eat me up?"

He's closer than you think! Wolfie said to himself, curling back his lips and showing his white fangs. *And he will gobble you up whole, little girl – shoes and socks and all!*

32

"You're right – it's very quiet in the woods," Hans observed, taking notice of Pearl's worries at last. He felt the hair at the back of his neck start to prickle.

"Stay close," Pearl told Hannah. "Hold my hand, let's run." She pictured Wolfie in every shadow, hiding behind every tree.

So Hans, Pearl and Hannah began to run along the path towards the stile.

Crouching low, moving stealthily, Wolfie followed. *Soon! Before they leave the wood, I will pounce!*

4

The sun had gone in behind the clouds when Hans's father set off for work with his axe over his shoulder.

"If you see Red Riding-Hood and her cousin Hannah, tell them to hurry home," Pearl's mother called from the door of the cottage. "The Duke has sent out an order for all children to stay indoors until his wife and son return to the castle."

Hans's father nodded. "It seems we are all to be punished," he grumbled, stepping out across the meadow.

He strode towards the stile, thinking of the work he must do – make firewood for his neighbours, chop logs, and fell the old ash tree at the back of Miller Brown's cottage. A busy day.

Over the stile and into the wood, wondering which job to do first, Hans's father was deep in thought. *The firewood!* he decided. *I know a small clearing close by, where the fallen wood is dry and good for burning.*

So he left the track and headed towards the river, smiling as he heard Hans's voice in the distance.

"'The grand old Duke of York,

He had ten thousand men . . .'"

And then, after a short while:

"'He marched them up to the top
of the hill

And he marched them down again!'"

"Hello!" Hans's father yelled through the trees. He turned back towards the path to meet up with his son.

Now or never! Wolfie thought. And he pounced.

Pearl, Hans and Hannah turned to see the huge grey creature leap out of the bushes, eyes flashing, teeth gnashing.

Hans and Pearl jumped in front of Hannah to protect her. Hans shielded them with his stick-sword.

Crack! Wolfie's powerful jaws split the twig in two. He snarled and threw himself at brave Hans.

"Son, where are you?" Hans's father raced through the wood. He could hear the snarls of the Wolf and Hannah's terrified cries.

"We're over here!" Pearl yelled as Hans grappled with Wolfie. "Hurry!"

The woodcutter raced through the wood, following the sounds. He found Pearl with her arms around Hannah and his son entangled with the grey brute. "Stand back!" he cried to the girls, and raised his axe.

Snap, snap! Wolfie's teeth bit into thin air as Hans ducked and dodged. He saw the blade of the axe above his head, felt it whistle by his whiskers as Hans's father crashed it down. *Thump!* The blade sank into the soft earth.

"Close, but not close enough!" Hans's dad muttered, raising the axe again.

Now Wolfie knew he was no match for the woodcutter and his axe. He would have to give up his breakfast and come back later for lunch. Leaping to one side, he avoided the second blow and, with a gnash of teeth, he sprinted away.

*

"Never, *never* go out in the woods alone!" Pearl's mother warned Hannah after their neighbour had walked Pearl and Hannah straight home. "Now that you've seen the Wolf, you understand why."

Hannah nodded.

"Not even to pick flowers or chase butterflies," Pearl's mother insisted. "And never visit your grandmother unless Red Riding-Hood goes with you."

"I promise," Hannah said, sitting beside Pearl on the doorstep to shell peas. *Pop!* went the pods, then the tiny peas rattled into the wooden bowl.

"Gertie will never forgive me if anything happens to the child," Pearl's mum sighed to herself. "Besides, we must obey the Duke's command to keep the children indoors. They say his temper has not improved since the Duchess left, and he spends all day hunting."

"Poor Stag," Pearl said, overhearing this last remark. "Let's hope the Duke doesn't get him with one of his horrible arrows."

She remembered her friend the stag bounding down the forest slopes into the open meadows, the Duke's hounds in hot pursuit. In the distance she thought she heard the cry of the hunters' horn and the howl of dogs. Shaking her head, she went on shelling peas.

All that day, Pearl and Hannah helped with chores around the house. They swept floors and polished tables, washed sheets and hung them out to dry. At midday

Hans arrived with firewood.

"No sign of Wolfie," he reported cheerfully. "I reckon my dad scared him off good and proper!"

"Back up to the mountain, we hope," Pearl said. "Well away from the village." But she couldn't help being afraid. After all, it was true what Amber had said before she came – they were reaching the part where Wolfie eats everybody up! *But it's me, not Hannah, that they should all be worried about*, she reminded herself. *Red Riding-Hood is the one Wolfie tries to scoff!*

It was teatime and the cottage was filled with the sweet smell of scones baking in the oven. The sun was sinking behind the mountain and the horns were calling for

41

the hunters to return to the castle.

"Yoo-hoo!" came the call from the meadow, and Hannah and Pearl ran to the door to see Gran approaching, carrying a large brown parcel tied with string. "Put the kettle on!" she cried. "Let me rest my weary bones!"

So the girls plumped up the cushions in the armchair and Pearl's mother made tea. Gran entered with a flurry of skirts and petticoats, putting down her parcel and whisking baby Tommy from his cradle. "How is my diddums, my darling!" she cooed, dandling him on her lap. "Who's my lovely little boy?"

Tommy gurgled then burped.

"Oops, pardon you!" Gran laughed, suddenly noticing the parcel on the table.

42

"That's for you, Hannah my precious. It's the present I said I'd make."

"Can I open it?" Hannah asked, her blue eyes shining.

"Of course. Let Red Riding-Hood help you with the string."

Hannah could hardly wait. Her fingers fumbled at the knots until Pearl loosened them for her. Then she tore open the paper.

"I made it to match the one I gave to Red Riding-Hood," Gran explained.

"Oh!" Hannah exclaimed as she held up her present – a long, red, hooded cloak.

"Put it on," Pearl's mum said. "How does it feel?"

"Lovely and warm," Hannah sighed. She pulled up the hood and let her grandmother tie the ribbons under her chin. "Now we look exactly the same!" she said to Pearl.

"Identical!" Gran laughed, as she stood back to admire her youngest granddaughter. "How will we tell you apart?"

For a moment, Hannah's small face looked puzzled then she came up with the answer. I know!" she cried, grasping Pearl's hand. "You can be *Big* Red Riding-Hood, and my name will be *Little* Red Riding-Hood! We'll go everywhere together, and the Wolf will never get us, so there!"

44

5

Uh-oh! Suddenly it all made sense. Here was Pearl, expecting to be the one who had to fight off Wolfie dressed up in Grandma's nightie and nightcap, and now it turned out not to be her at all, but Hannah!

I'd never have let Wolfie's lame disguise fool me, Pearl said to herself as little Hannah gave a twirl and her new red cloak

45

billowed out. *But Hannah's young – she might get taken in by Wolfie's "All the better to see you with" stuff.*

"Why so quiet?" Hans asked Pearl as he dashed in through the door. "Hey, nice cloak!" he said, turning to Hannah. Then back to Pearl. "I've just seen some cows hanging over your back garden fence," he whispered. "It looks like they want to talk."

So Pearl slipped quietly out of the cottage and went to have a word with the three gentle brown cows with the big dark eyes and broad pink noses. "Is something wrong?" she asked anxiously.

One of the cows shook her head. "No, but we heard from the sparrow who-oo flew from the wood that the kingfisher

had been told by the owl that Stag wishes to speak with you-oo!"

Pearl knew the message must be important. "Where is Stag?" she asked.

"By the stile at the edge of the wood," the second cow told her. "Go quickly, before the sun sets."

So, without telling anyone where she was going, Pearl set off across the meadow. When she came to the stile she stopped and called Stag's name.

"Hush!" A long-eared hare appeared

from behind a tree. He made Pearl jump. "The stag cannot stay in the open for fear of the Wolf, who lurks somewhere in the wood."

"Will you take me to him?" Pearl asked, darting quick looks into the gathering shadows.

The hare nodded. "Go gently. Make no sound."

So Pearl followed deep into the wood, glad to see the owl perched on a high branch, watching their progress.

"Not far now!" Owl hooted. "Don't be afraid, Red Riding-Hood. We'll loo-ook out for the Wolf and warn yoo-ou if he comes near!"

"Thanks!" Pearl whispered as she bent low to follow the hare through a thicket of young willows into a clearing where her noble friend the stag was waiting.

"Ah, Red Riding-Hood!" Stag seemed pleased to see her. He stood with his head high, his magnificent antlers brushing against the canopy of green leaves. "I bring news from the creatures of the forest high above the castle – the fox and the eagle have spoken!"

Pearl ventured close to the beautiful stag. She could tell from the matted fur around his neck and from his thin flanks that he had run far and eaten little. "I heard the Duke and his men out hunting earlier," she murmured. "I was afraid they would catch you."

"It has been a hard day," Stag admitted. "But the news I bring offers hope to all those creatures whom the Duke hunts down with his bow and arrow."

Pearl's worries lifted when she heard this. "Tell me quickly!" she begged. "And I'll do whatever I can to help."

"The news is this. This afternoon the eagle flew over the mountain to the place where the Duchess stays."

"At her mother's house," Pearl nodded. "Everyone knows that she had a big fight with the Duke and left him."

"The eagle soared over the courtyard where two women walked and talked, and the baby cried."

Poor Max! Pearl thought. Her gran was right – she really was the only person who could keep him happy.

"Eagle heard the old woman say to her

daughter that it was her duty to return to her husband. The young woman cried that she would not, unless her husband the Duke agreed to one condition."

Pearl nodded eagerly. How cool that the eagle could fly and soar and discover what was going on for miles around!

"The Duchess said that she was fed-up of staying in the castle all day while her husband rode out with his men. She told her mother that if the Duke were to give up hunting and stay with her and make her life pleasant, then she would return!"

"That's amazing!" Pearl gasped. "How brilliant would that be for you and all the other deer in the forest?"

"But the Duchess is proud," Stag reminded her. "She told her mother that not only must the Duke give up hunting, but he must come to her on bended knee and beg forgiveness."

"That's a tough one," Pearl muttered. The last she heard, the Duke was storming around the palace in the worst of moods. She didn't see him doing the bended knee thing in the near future.

"So the eagle brought this news back over the mountain top," Stag went on. "He told it to the fox, who raced down the mountainside to tell it to the hare who ran to tell me, and so we came together to find you."

"To ask me for help?" Pearl asked, still unsure about what she could do.

Stag paused for a while then spoke again. "People are strange creatures, full of jealousies and anger. It is hard for me to understand."

"So you want me to think of a way to make the Duke sorry enough to give up hunting and go and ask the Duchess to come home?" *That's a tough one*, Pearl thought. *Who can talk sense into the angry Duke?*

"Well?" Stag asked, looking deep into Pearl's eyes.

She was under pressure, desperately seeking an answer, when one name suddenly popped into her head.

"Gran!" she cried, seeing the whole thing in a flash. "Don't worry," she told Stag, turning for home. "If anyone can do this, Gran can!"

6

"Follow me!" the hare said to Pearl.

He led the way, guided by the squirrels and the rabbits of the wood.

"The Wolf is behind you!" the rabbits warned. "Beyond the stream, following silently."

So the hare led Pearl swiftly away from the stream, cutting through the trees so that Pearl could catch no glimpse of the

meadow or the village beyond.

"Scary!" she muttered, putting her trust in the animals.

"Now the Wolf is sneaking ahead of you!" the squirrels warned from their tree-tops. "Quickly – you must turn away towards the river."

Startled, the hare changed direction again. "Run fast!" he muttered to Pearl.

"The Wolf is swift and may pounce at any time."

"Straight ahead!" the rabbits cried. "There is the stile. Wolfie will not follow you into the meadow!"

Pearl scrambled over the stile and jumped clear of the woods into the long, cool grass.

"Safe from my grasp for now!" Wolfie grumbled as Pearl escaped. He lay panting at the edge of the wood, cursing and watching her go.

"Here goes!" Pearl muttered. She flung open the cottage door and found her grandmother sitting by the fire with Hannah, teaching her how to sew.

"Make neat stitches with your needle,"

Gran said. "In and out, in and out."

"Guess what!" Pearl cried. "I just heard a rumour about the Duchess!"

Of course, Pearl had to touch up the truth a little. She made no mention of the stag or the hare, the cows, the eagle or the owl. Instead, "A herdsman on the far side of the mountain overheard the Duchess talking to her mother," she told Gran. "He said the Duchess already longs to return home, only she can't bear the Duke to go out hunting, besides, she's too proud to admit that she misses him."

"Aha!" Gran cried, her eyes lighting up. "I knew the Duchess would not keep baby Max away from his father for long. This is good news indeed."

"But who can persuade His Grace the

Duke to give up his beloved hunting?" Pearl asked, full of fake innocence, her eyes fixed on Gran. "It would have to be a very brave person . . ."

"Who can pick on his weak spot." With a wink at Pearl, quick-witted Hans took up the argument. "Someone who knows the Duke well."

"Someone like you, Gran!" Pearl said, as if she had only just thought of it.

"Me?" For a split second her grandmother hesitated. Then she clapped her hands and stood up, letting Hannah's sewing fall to the floor. "Of course! I'm the one! Give me my cloak, lend me a lantern, I will go at once to the castle!"

With difficulty Pearl's mum persuaded

Pearl's grandmother to wait until the next day. "Let the Duke sleep on it," she advised. "Leave him to his loneliness for one more night."

So Pearl's gran stayed over at the cottage and was up with the lark, rousing Pearl and Hannah to walk with her to the Duke's castle.

"Come on, little dormice, wake up!" she cried, loud enough to rouse the cockerel in Farmer Meade's yard.

Cock-a-doodle-doo! he cried, strutting out on to the empty village street.

Pearl and Hannah rolled sleepily out of bed, dressed quickly and put on their matching red cloaks.

Out in the wood, Wolfie opened one eye then went back to sleep.

"Off we go!" Gran urged the girls out of the cottage into the misty morning.

Along the street they went, past the strutting cockerel, up the hill, climbing the steps to the castle.

Rat-a-tat-tat! Gran knocked loudly at the door. "Open up!" she cried.

A sleepy servant opened the door. He'd slept in the stable to keep out of the Duke's way and his clothes were covered in straw.

"Here we are to look after His Baby Grace!" Gran announced with a wide smile. "I've brought my two granddaughters to play with Max. Come on, man, step out of our way!"

"But didn't you hear?" The servant cast a scared glance over his shoulder. "Her Grace the Duchess – she – er – oh dear!"

Hearing the approach of loud footsteps, the dishevelled servant bolted.

"What is it?" the Duke demanded. He stood hands on hips, barring the way. "What do you want, woman? Why are you here?"

Pearl took one look at the Duke's unshaven face and shuddered. His eyes

were red, as if he hadn't slept a wink, and his clothes were wrinkled.

"We are here to entertain the noble baby," Gran answered steadily. "I am his nurse, Your Grace. And these dear, sweet children are my granddaughters."

"You fool – haven't you heard that my wife and son have left me?" the Duke roared.

Pearl and Hannah quaked in their shoes.

"Left you, Your Grace?" Pearl's gran exclaimed, pushing boldly past the Duke and looking around the courtyard. "But no doubt they will be back soon."

The Duke heaved an impatient sigh. "Guards!" he called. "Throw this woman and these girls into the dungeon!"

Luckily for them, no guard was brave enough to appear.

"Nonsense," Gran argued. "We have no time for games, Your Grace. Tell me when your son will return. My girls are longing to play."

For a moment Pearl thought that the Duke was going to seize Gran and throw her in jail himself. But instead, she saw the harsh lines of his harsh face crumple and tears come to his eyes.

"My wife and my son have gone for ever," he confessed. "And, good Nurse, I am at a loss without them!"

7

"This is what you must do to get your son back," Pearl's gran told the Duke.

She, Pearl and Hannah sat with him in the banquet hall. The Duke had scared the servants off so thoroughly that empty dishes, bread crusts, fish bones and oyster shells were still strewn across the long table. Ashes from burnt out logs were heaped in the huge grate.

Talking about baby Max had done it, Pearl realised. Gran had found the Duke's weak spot and prised him open like one of the oyster shells.

"You must be ready to say sorry to Her Grace the Duchess."

The Duke sat amongst the wreckage of his grand hall. "Sorry for what?" he asked simply.

"Why, sorry for leaving her alone all day while you ride out to hunt," Pearl's grandmother explained. "Your Grace must surely realise that a woman does not marry and have a son so that her husband may desert them for his companions and the thrill of the chase!"

"True," the Duke mumbled. "I have not taken enough care of them."

"But a woman's nature is to forgive," Gran continued wisely as the Duke hung on every word. "A man only has to go down on his knee to say sorry before she flies back into his arms."

Whoa, which century are we in? Pearl couldn't help wondering. *Oh that's it – I forgot – we're in Red Riding-Hood century!*

"I will apologise!" the Duke resolved, standing up from the table. "Call my groom. Tell him I will ride over the mountain this very minute!"

Pearl's grandmother nodded and smiled. "Very well, Your Grace. And tell Her Grace, the Duchess that we will be here, ready to take care of Max the moment he returns."

*

Pearl and Hannah spent all day helping their grandmother and the castle servants clean and make everything ready.

"The Duke will say sorry to the Duchess!" the whisper ran down the corridors to the kitchen, up the stairs to the bedrooms and the nursery. "He will promise never to hunt again!"

Pearl grinned at Hannah and thought how brilliant the stag's life would be from now on – grazing in forest clearings and drinking from sparkling streams instead of having to flee the hounds and the Duke's arrows.

But the palace servants still found room to grumble. "And now the Duchess will return victorious, more proud than ever," the chambermaids muttered.

"Life is never perfect," Gran told them, plumping up Max's lace pillows. "We must smile and curtsey and keep well out of reach of Her Grace's sharp tongue. Hannah, my dear, lay out Max's clean clothes. Pearl, make sure that the window is open to let in the fresh air."

That evening, the Duchess returned to the castle in a shiny purple coach decorated with gold. She took the Duke's hand and stepped out with baby Max in her arms. Rings of amethyst sparkled on her fingers and her lace collar was finer than ever.

"Prepare a bath for the baby!" she ordered Pearl's grandmother. "Use only water perfumed with lavender and the softest towels."

Meanwhile, the Duke sent his huntsmen to their homes beyond the forest. He snapped his hunting bow in two and threw it on the fire.

"Hurray!" Pearl whispered to Hannah.

"Happy now?" Gran winked as she whisked baby Max off for his bath. "By the way, the Duchess has asked me to stay here for the night. Red Riding-Hood, you must take Hannah by the hand and lead her home as fast as you can."

*

"It's OK – everyone can relax," Pearl announced to the hare waiting at the castle gate. "The Duke has given up hunting – it's official!"

The hare stood tall on his hind legs. "Wait until the stag hears this!" he cried. "I will pass on the news. It will spread like wildfire!"

"Huh!" a grumpy voice said as Pearl and Hannah set off down the steps. "Typical – not even a 'Hello, how are you?'"

"Ratty?" Pearl asked, peering to either side of the path.

"Down here," he muttered, "in the gutter where I belong."

She spied him beside a heap of dry leaves. While Hannah went off to pick violets, Pearl bent down to speak to him. "Hey, don't be like that – I didn't know you were there."

"Obviously not." The rat was in a sulk. "I've been around all day, if you had but chosen to look. In the kitchen, on the stairs, hiding behind the curtains in the nursery . . ."

"Sorry!" Pearl meant it. The rat might be grumpy, but he was always there when she needed him. "I have to take Hannah home before it gets dark," she explained. "We've had a brilliant day. No more hunting – ta-dah!"

"I'm always the last to know," Ratty grumbled. "No one pays me any attention. I'm only a rat, after all. And by the way, take care the child doesn't

wander too far
and trip over that
log . . . tut, too late!"
"Help!" Hannah cried,
tumbling down the hill and
spilling her bunch of purple
flowers. "Red Riding-Hood, I'm falling.
Catch me . . . ouch!"

8

"I asked you to take good care of Hannah," Pearl's mum grumbled at Pearl as she wiped porridge from Tommy's face after breakfast next morning. "And what happens? The poor child comes back covered in mud, with her new cloak all torn!"

"I tripped and fell down the mountain," Hannah explained. "It wasn't Red

Riding-Hood's fault."

"In any case, you must take needle and thread and mend the tear before your grandmamma sees it," Pearl's mum decided.

"I'll do it later," Pearl said hurriedly. Mending wasn't her strong point. In fact, she wouldn't know where to begin.

"Now," her mother said firmly. Then she turned to Hannah, drew her close and spoke in a warm, soft voice. "Come here, my dear. I have some news for you. Your mother has finished her business in town."

Hannah gasped and her eyes lit up. "Where's Mummy? Can I see her?"

"Tomorrow," Pearl's mother explained. "You will sleep here for one more night and in the morning I will take you home."

Thank goodness for that! Pearl thought. Looking after Hannah and keeping her safe from Wolfie had been pretty stressful.

"Why not now?" Hannah asked impatiently.

"Tomorrow," Pearl's mother insisted. "Today I'll go to your house and get everything ready for your mother's arrival. Red Riding-Hood will stay here with you."

Rats! Pearl thought. *One more day of worry!*

But there was no way out of it as Pearl's mum filled her basket with bread, milk and butter and set off with Tommy for Gertie's house.

*

In the cottage Hannah fidgeted and fussed. She went to the window and stared out then squirmed and wriggled when Pearl put her red cloak around her shoulders and tried to fix the tear.

"How can I mend it if you won't stand still?" Pearl asked, clumsily pricking her finger with the needle. "Ouch!"

"Is it bedtime yet?" Hannah fretted. "When will it be morning?"

Pearl's finger was bleeding. She went out to the pump in the back garden to wash it clean. When she hurried back inside, Hannah wasn't there.

"Hannah?" Pearl called upstairs. "Where are you?"

There was no answer. "Come down, Hannah. I'm not playing hide and seek

76

with you. We have to mend your cloak!"

Still no reply, so Pearl dashed out into the street, calling Hannah's name.

Lydia East heard her and came to her cottage door.

"Have you seen Hannah?" Pearl cried. "I turned my back for a moment and now she's gone!"

Their neighbour frowned. "I'm sorry, Red Riding-Hood, I haven't seen her. But try Farmer Meade, who passed by just now with his cart."

Pearl ran down the road to the farmyard gate. "Have you seen my cousin Hannah?" she asked. "She's dressed in her new red cloak, so you can't mistake her."

Farmer Meade had been to market. He was unloading empty baskets from his cart. "No, there was no sign of her on the road," he told Pearl. "Try the village green."

Pearl's heart thudded fast and furiously as she ran and searched the green. Anxiously she went down to the duck pond and asked the ducks, not caring who saw her or overheard. "I'm looking for my cousin, Hannah," she gasped, down on her hands and knees. "Did she come this way?"

The ducks swam in small, agitated circles. "We would love to help," they told Pearl, quacking softly. "But we have not seen the child. She did not come this way."

"She can't just vanish!" Pearl cried, jumping up and running back home. "Hannah, stop hiding! This isn't a game. Come out, wherever you are!"

*

But Hannah *had* vanished and Pearl felt hollow with fear. She had looked everywhere, asked everyone, and still there was no sign.

Think! Pearl told herself as she tried to stop her heart racing and her mind whirling. *Think back to when it happened. Try to figure out where Hannah would go! Remember, she was wishing time would fly, longing for tomorrow. She couldn't wait to see her mum.*

"What would innocent little Hannah do? Who would she want to share her good news with?" Pearl muttered, staring up the hill. "Of course!" she said suddenly. "That's where she is – she's run up to the castle to tell Gran!"

*

"Hannah!" Hurriedly Pearl put on her cloak to follow her cousin. She called her name as she ran up the hill.

A swallow swooped low. "I will fly ahead and search for the child," she promised, soaring on.

"Have you seen my cousin, *Little* Red Riding-Hood?" Pearl asked the fox who crossed her path.

"I'm busy hunting for food for my cubs," the fox replied. "Nevertheless I will help you in your search." And she ran swiftly up the hill, on the lookout for a small girl in a red cloak.

At last Pearl reached the castle steps. She raced up two at a time and knocked loudly on the door.

"Yes?" The servant who had slept in the

stables was back to his smart, snooty self. "What do you want?"

"I'm looking for Little Red Riding-Hood," Pearl gasped. "Please let me in."

The servant looked down his nose at the breathless visitor. He had orders from the Duke to let no one in except the dressmaker bringing new gowns for the Duchess. "Go away!" he told Pearl. And he slammed the door in her face.

9

Helplessly Pearl hammered her fists against the door but the servant did not return.

"Let me in!" she cried, so long and loud that it brought a familiar face into view.

"Hello, hello!" Ratty exclaimed as he scuttled out of some nearby bushes. "I wondered who was making that dreadful din!"

"Am I pleased to see you!" Pearl exclaimed. "The Duke's servant slammed the door in my face and I so *have* to get in. Maybe you can help me!"

"Oh, I see things are different now," the rat replied, carefully stroking his whiskers. "Yesterday you had no need of me and so you ignored me."

Pearl shook her head. "I didn't mean . . . I wasn't . . . I'm sorry, Rat. I really am!"

Her furry friend tutted. "Just because I keep to the shadows and take care not to get in the way doesn't mean I like to be ignored," he huffed. "We rats may live in the dungeons and come and go by a secret

83

entrance, but we still have feelings that can be hurt."

"What's that about a secret entrance?" Pearl interrupted eagerly. Then she took a deep breath. "Rat, if I say sorry about yesterday – and I am, truly, truly – will you please show me the secret way into the castle?"

The rat eyed her sternly. "You're far too big to squeeze through the gap," he said. "But come this way – I'll show you."

So Pearl followed the rat around the side of the castle, its high walls looming overhead. "Hurry!" she whispered. "I've lost my cousin Hannah. I have an idea that she ran all the way up here to see our grandmother!"

Ratty stopped in his tracks. "You mean

the small child with golden curls who was here yesterday?" he checked.

Pearl nodded. "She's *Little* Red Riding-Hood, and she knows that Gran stayed here overnight. I expect she ran to the castle to tell her the good news about her mother."

"Why didn't you say so earlier, instead of wasting everybody's time?" Ratty complained, squatting on his haunches and refusing to budge.

"What do you mean?" A fresh panic seized hold of Pearl.

"Calm down," Ratty insisted. "I'm telling you that your cousin would not find your grandmother even if she came this way."

"Why's that?" Pearl almost cried with

frustration, waiting for the rat's slow reply.

"For one thing, the doorman who slammed the door in your face would most certainly have slammed it in your cousin's face too."

Hannah groaned. "I hadn't thought of that."

"For another thing, your grandmother isn't here," Ratty explained, his beady eyes fixed on Pearl.

"But she is!" Pearl cried. "The Duchess asked her to stay last night to look after Max!"

"Hush!" The rat raised a warning paw and squinted upwards in case a sentry was passing along the battlements. "Your grandmother *was* here last night, but she *isn't* any longer. She left at dawn in the

86

Duchess's purple carriage. I know this for a fact because I watched her go."

There was no point arguing with Ratty – Pearl knew he wouldn't lie. But his news made her heart sink. "What do I do now?" she sighed.

"Don't give in!" the grey doves cooed. They were perched on the high wall above Pearl's head.

"Who's giving in?" Ratty snapped crossly. "We're not so easily put off the track, are we, Red Riding-Hood?"

"You're right – no way!" Quickly Pearl gathered her courage and looked down at the rat. "You said 'we'. Does that mean you'll help me?"

"Of course. What are friends for?" he replied. "And listen; if I'd known that you were searching for the child, I would have stopped her and sent her straight back to you."

Pearl stared at him. "You *saw* her?"

Ratty nodded and set off briskly down the hill. "As clear as day," he answered. "Earlier this morning. She was in the wood by the meadow, running as fast as her little legs would carry her. Come, follow me!"

Hannah stood in the middle of the wood in her bright red cloak. "Which is the way to Grandmamma's house?" she wondered to herself.

"Turn back, Little Red Riding-Hood!" the squirrels chattered from way above. "Your grandmother isn't at home!"

But Hannah didn't hear them.

"Is this the path? Or is this it?" She went a few steps deeper into the wood then turned again. All around, the trees grew tall and tangled. No sunlight shone through. "Help, where am I?" Hannah cried.

She had seized the moment and hurried from the cottage when Red Riding-Hood had been busy, eager to share her wonderful news. *I'll run to find Grandmamma in her cottage. She'll be happy for me!* Without remembering where her grandmother had spent the night,

Hannah had run across the sunny meadow, over the stile and into the wood.

But shadows had gathered and the path grew hard to follow. Soon she was lost. And she was very small and alone in the big wood.

*

Good things come to those who wait! Wolfie thought, creeping nearer to the lonely figure. He couldn't believe his luck. There he had been, basking in the sun by the river, when he'd heard the young squirrels' warning cries: "Turn back, Little Red Riding-Hood! Your grandmother isn't at home!"

Oh-ho! he'd thought. *Here comes breakfast!*

And he'd got up and stretched and licked his lips.

And now here she was! Wolfie had stalked through the trees and found Hannah with ease – the pretty young child in the red cloak.

"Help!" she cried, turning this way and that. "Where am I?"

Lost! thought Wolfie, licking his lips. *And best of all, alone!*

10

Pearl's grandmother was a happy woman as she sat on the silk cushions in the Duchess's purple coach. *All's well that ends well!* she thought, leaning out of the window and waving graciously at Farmer Meade as they drove down the village street. *The Duke and Duchess are friends once more and I have His Baby Grace back in my arms!*

"Dear Nurse, take the coach," the Duchess had said. "Return home for fresh clothes for yourself and stop at the market on your way back to the castle. Buy sugar plums for Max!"

So Gran had set off in style, ordering the coachman to drive through the village so that everyone could see her in her finery. "Now turn left by the village green!" she called from inside the coach. "Drive along the track around the edge of the wood. We must not keep His Baby Grace waiting. Hurry, man, hurry!"

Pearl had never run so fast or so far. Down the hill into the village, past Farmer Meade and Lydia East, past her own front door and on into the meadow.

"You must slow down!" Ratty panted as he scuttled under the stile into the wood. "My legs are too short to keep up!"

"Aunt Gertie will never forgive me if something bad happens to Hannah!" Pearl gasped. "Come to that – I'll never forgive *myself*!"

"Very well, Red Riding-Hood, run on ahead!" Ratty cried, huffing and puffing. "But look there, leaning against that tree – a woodcutter's axe! Seize it and carry it with you!"

Pearl nodded and took the rat's advice. You never knew in this dark wood when an axe would come in useful.

*

"I'm lost!" Hannah cried, walking round and round in circles. It seemed the wood was full of creatures scuffling and twigs snapping, wind blowing and shadows moving. "Grandmamma, where are you?"

So that's where you're bound! sly Wolfie thought. He was close on Hannah's heels, hiding in the bushes. *To the cosy four walls of your grandmother's house.*

By good luck Hannah spied an opening between the trees and she followed it. The wood opened out at last. The shadows lifted and she saw Miller Brown's tall mill ahead, with her grandmother's cottage nestled beside it. "At last!" she cried, setting off as fast as she could. "Grandmamma, it's me – Little Red Riding-Hood. Come out and listen to my news!"

Oh no you don't! Wolfie thought, secretly streaking ahead to overtake the tasty child. *I'll be there long before you and waiting for you with my sharp teeth and claws at the ready, my dear!*

Inside the cottage Gran folded a fresh nightdress and nightcap and laid them on her bed. She was glad she'd sent the coachman on ahead to market to buy the sugar plums. Now she had time to relax and get herself ready to return to the castle.

"'Diddle-diddle dumpling, my son John!'" she hummed. "'Went to bed with his trousers on . . .'"

Wolfie burst roaring through the bedroom door. He seized a shawl hanging

96

on the back of the door, gagged Gran and tied her up before she even had time to scream. He shoved her in the wardrobe, locked the door and threw away the key – da-dah!

Then he grabbed the clean nightdress and nightcap laid out on the bed and slipped them on.

Now into bed! he crowed, jumping in and pulling the covers up to his chin. *And let the fun begin!*

"Grandmamma!" Hannah knocked at the door. She knocked again. "It's me, Little Red Riding-Hood!"

"Come in!" a feeble voice called from upstairs.

Hannah opened the door and went up

to her grandmother's bedroom. "What's the matter, Grandmamma? Are you poorly?" she asked.

"Very poorly, child," Wolfie replied, hiding his vicious grin behind the sheets. "You must come closer!"

"Guess what – Mummy's coming home tomorrow!" Hannah began, wondering a little about the strange knocking coming from inside the wardrobe. Then she gasped at the long furry ears peeking out from under her gran's nightcap. "Why,

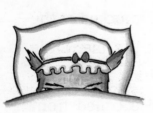 Grandmamma, what big ears you have!"

"All the better to hear you with!" Wolfie cackled.

Come closer, simpleton, until I can reach out and snap you up!

Hannah crept closer. "One more night and Mummy will be home," she reported, startled by her gran's staring yellow eyes. "Why, Grandmamma, what big eyes you have!"

"All the better to see you with!" Wolfie croaked. *To see those plump cheeks and pink skin – yum-yum!* He  couldn't help it – he just had to keep on grinning at the tasty prospect. The covers slipped and showed his gleaming fangs.

 "Why, Grandmamma!" Hannah cried, seriously scared. "What big teeth you have!"

"All the better to . . ." Wolfie threw back the bedclothes and leaped out of bed in

Gran's long nightdress ". . . gobble you up!"

"Oh no, you don't!" Super-Pearl cried, bounding into the room with her red cloak flying. She waved the axe above her head. Beneath his fur, Wolfie turned deadly pale. He tripped over the long nightie as he tried to sidestep the swipe of Pearl's axe. *Oof!* He landed flat on his face.

"You devil!" Gran cried as she broke free from the wardrobe with a mighty crash. She seized the umbrella by her bed and began to beat Wolfie. "Take that . . . and that . . . and that!"

Wolfie lay on the floor as the blows rained down. "Now hit him with the axe!" Gran cried, standing to one side at last.

Her arms trembling with the weight, Pearl raised the weapon. *Yuck!* she thought, hesitating for a split second before she splatted Wolfie.

Just long enough for him to jump up and leap out of the window. He landed smack on his face. *Oof-ooch!*

Then he was up and off in Gran's best nightie, straight into the whirling sails of the miller's windmill which raised him high in the air then dumped him on the ground – *whack-crack!* Staggering on without looking where he was going, Wolfie fell into the deep millpond – *splash!*

"Good riddance and don't come back!" Gran cried from her bedroom window.

Pearl and Hannah heard Wolfie howl as he sank below the surface – once, twice, three times! *Ow-oow! Ow-oow! Ow-oow!*

11

"It is you we have to thank, Red Riding-Hood," the stag told Pearl as he walked her and Hannah back through the wood.

Wolfie had drowned in the millpond and there were only small bubbles rising to the surface when Ratty had arrived on the scene with Stag.

"Never to be seen again!" Ratty said with a satisfied smile at his antlered friend.

"What did I say – Red Riding-Hood was more than a match for the Wolf!"

Gran had dusted her hands together and carried on packing as if nothing had happened. "Leave the wardrobe door where it is," she'd told Pearl. "I'll chop it up for firewood when I get the chance." Then she'd hugged Hannah and said she was happy to hear her news, and for her to be a good girl for her mummy, and goodbye because the Duchess was waiting, and the coachman was back with sugar plums for His Baby Grace.

"Bye!" Pearl and Hannah had stood in her doorway in their matching red cloaks, waving her off.

Magic! Pearl had thought. *What a totally cool gran!*

Now she was getting ready to say other goodbyes as they came to the stile at the edge of the wood.

"Life will be peaceful here without the Wolf and without the Duke's hunters," Stag told her in his deep, kindly voice.

"Peaceful for some," Ratty grumbled. "Others such as I will go on in the gutter as before!"

Pearl smiled and knelt down to shake his paw. "Thank you, Ratty – for everything. And goodbye."

Ratty blinked shyly then coughed. "Um – er, goodbye. Until we meet again." Then he hurried off into the ditch.

"And goodbye, Stag," Pearl said sadly.

The wise creature gazed at her. "Farewell," he murmured before he turned and walked slowly into the wood. "Go well through life, Red Riding-Hood."

Pearl sighed and watched him go.

"While we're on with the final farewells, here's one from me," Hans told Pearl, suddenly stepping out from behind a nearby woodpile. "Come on, shake hands with me before you go."

"I – I'm not going anywhere right now," Pearl stammered, though she knew her time in Red Riding-Hood world was coming to an end.

"Shake anyway," Hans insisted.

So Pearl took his hand and smiled. "Thanks for everything," she murmured.

Then Hannah spied Pearl's mother trudging with Tommy along the village street and she ran across the meadow to greet her. "Is it time for bed?" she cried. "Is it nearly tomorrow?"

And suddenly Pearl felt so tired that she had to sit down by the stile and lean against it in the last rays of the sun, letting her eyelids droop until she felt she was drifting off into a deep sleep.

And *whoosh!* The bright light shone and she was gone.

*

"Wake up!" Lily tugged the sleeve of Pearl's frilly nightdress. "You were ages."

Slowly Pearl opened her eyes. The sparkling light was fading. Everything was going back to normal here in Amber's basement. But inside her head she was still half back in Red Riding-Hood world.

"You look dazed," Amber said, helping her to her feet. "Are you OK? Wolfie didn't dress up in Gran's nightie and try to scoff you, did he?"

"Not exactly," Pearl said with a grin. Her head cleared and she looked forward to taking her time and telling Lily and Pearl the whole truth. "Actually, it was a lot more complicated than that . . ."

Have you checked out...

www.dressingupdreams.net

It's the place to go for games, downloads, activities, sneak previews and lots of fun!

You'll find a special dressing-up game and lots of activities and fun things to do, as well as news on Dressing-Up Dreams and all your favourite characters.

Sign up to the newsletter at **www.dressingupdreams.net** to receive extra clothes for your Dressing-Up Dreams doll and the opportunity to enter special members only competitions.

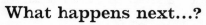

What happens next...?
Log onto www.dressingupdreams.net for a sneak preview of my next adventure!

COLOURING FUN!

Carefully colour the Dressing-Up Dreams picture
on the next page and then send it in to us.

Or you can draw your very own fairytale
character. You might want to think about what
they would wear or if they have special powers.

Each month, we will put the best entries
on the website gallery and one lucky winner
will receive a magical Dressing-Up Dreams
goodie bag!

Send your drawing,
your name, age and address on a postcard to:
Pearl's Dressing-Up Dreams Competition

UK Readers:
Hodder Children's Books
338 Euston Road
London NW1 3BH
kidsmarketing@hodder.co.uk

Australian Readers:
Hachette Children's Books
Level 17/207 Kent Street
Sydney NSW 2000
childrens.books@hachette.com.au

New Zealand Readers:
Hachette Livre NZ L
PO Box 100 749
North Shore City 07
childrensbooks@hachette

WIN A Dressing-Up Dreams GOODIE BAG!

CAN YOU SPOT THE TWO DIFFERENCES AND THE HIDDEN LETTER IN THESE TWO PICTURES OF PEARL

There is a spot-the-difference picture and hidden letter in the back of all f
Dressing-Up Dreams books about Pearl (look for the books with
9 to 12 on the spine). Hidden in one of the pictures above is a secret lette
Find all four letters and put them together to make a special Dressing-U
Dreams word, then send it to us. Each month, we will put the correct entr
in a draw and one lucky winner will receive a magical Dressing-Up Drean
goodie bag including an exclusive Dressing-Up Dreams keyring!

Send your magical word, your name, age and your address
on a postcard to: **Pearl's Dressing-Up Dreams Competition**

UK Readers:	**Australian Readers:**	**New Zealand Reade**
Hodder Children's Books	Hachette Children's Books	Hachette Livre NZ
338 Euston Road	Level 17/207 Kent Street	PO Box 100 749
London NW1 3BH	Sydney NSW 2000	North Shore City 0
kidsmarketing@hodder.co.uk	childrens.books@hachette.com.au	childrensbooks@hachett

Only one entry per child. Final draw: 30th March 2010
For full terms and conditions go to http://www.hodderchildrens.co.uk/Terms_and_Conditions.ht